DRAGON ROCK

by Jack D. Clifford

Illustrated by Russ Daff

W
FRANKLIN WATTS
LONDON•SYDNEY

Ed and Lia were playing a game.

They were looking for dragon eggs in a magical valley.

"I see a dragon's nest!" shouted Ed.

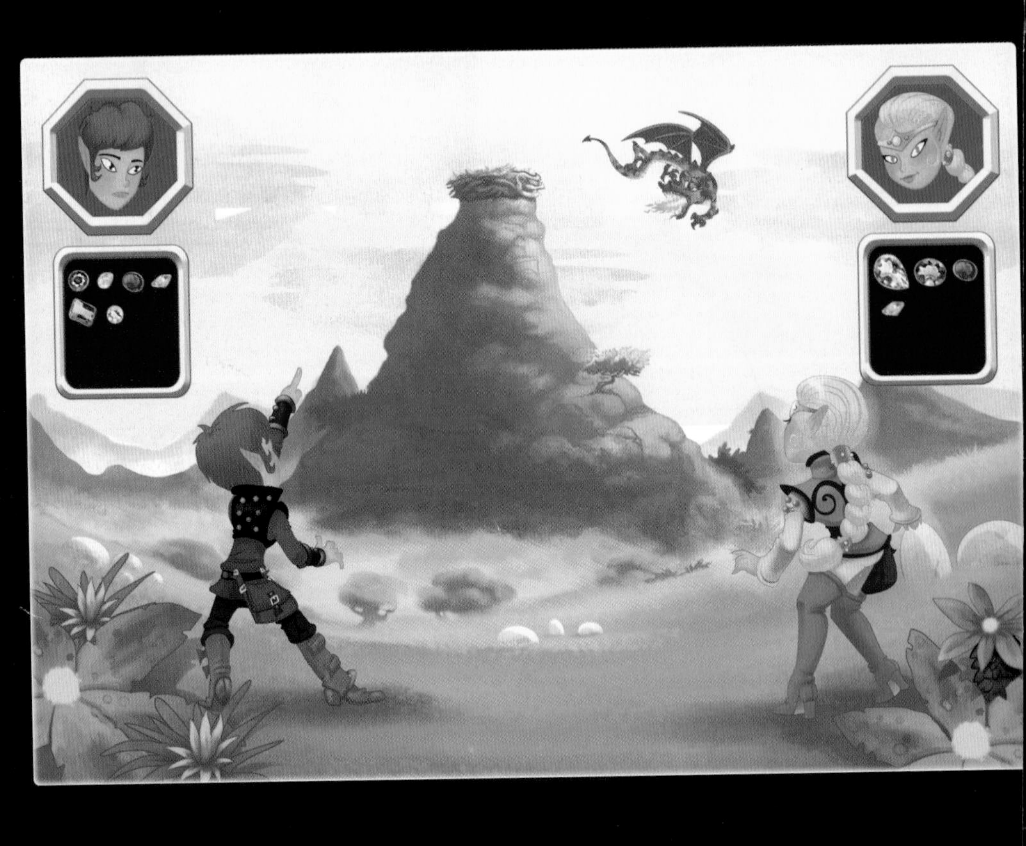

Suddenly, a red light shone ...

Ed and Lia were in a green valley!

“Where are we?” asked Lia.

“I think we’re in the game,” cried Ed.

“Isn’t that the dragon’s nest?”

“Yes,” said Lia. “We should watch out for trolls!”

Suddenly, something enormous flew above them. Then a piercing screech shattered the air.

A dragon swooped down and landed nearby. Ed and Lia crouched down low as the dragon picked up stones and sniffed around.

"The dragon looks like it's searching for something!" whispered Ed.

"Perhaps it's lost an egg!" said Lia.

The dragon flew back up to the nest,

dropping stones all the way.

Just then, the bushes began to shake.

A huge hand scooped them up.

“TROLL!” screamed Ed and Lia.

“Ha ha!” boomed the troll.

“I’ll put you with my stones!”

The troll tucked them into his pocket.

There were lots of stones inside it.

“Ed!” said Lia. “This one feels warm. It can’t be a stone. It’s the dragon’s egg.”

"We must get it back to the dragon's nest," said Ed.

"How?" asked Lia.

"The dragon left a trail of stones all the way up the rock," said Ed.

“So we need to make the troll follow the trail!” said Lia.

Ed and Lia found a sharp stone and cut a hole in the troll's pocket. They pushed the stone through ...

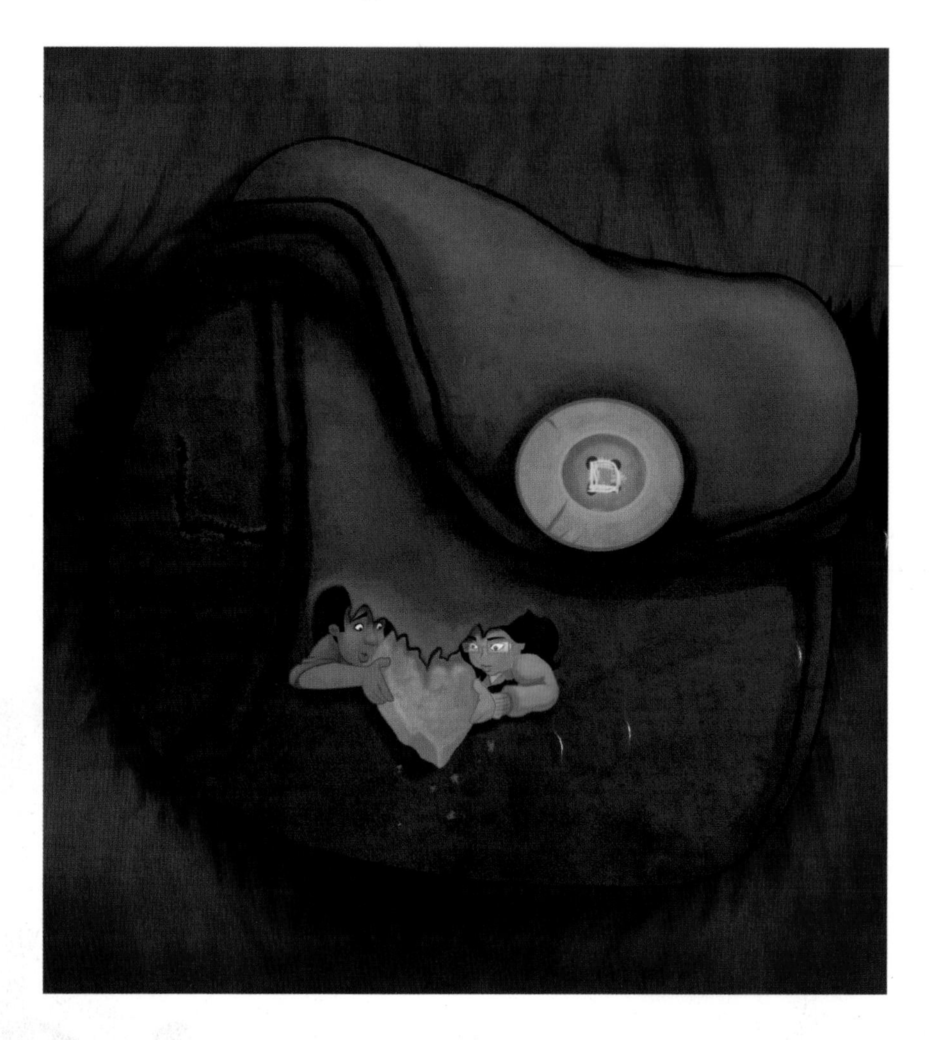

… so it landed on the troll's toe.

"Ouch!" yelped the troll, looking down.

"Oh! More stones!"

The troll followed the stone trail

up the steep rock.

Ed and Lia protected the egg as more and more stones crashed into the pocket.

At last, the troll clambered up

near the dragon's nest.

Carefully, Lia and Ed rolled the egg out of the troll's pocket. Then they jumped down beside it.

At that moment came the piercing cry of the mother dragon coming back. The troll fled back down the rock.

Suddenly, the egg began to crack.

"Time to go!" yelled Ed.

A red light shone ...

... and they were back home.

“Egg-cellent game!” laughed Lia.

PUZZLE TIME

Can you put these pictures

in the correct order?

TURN OVER FOR ANSWERS!

Tell the story in your own words

with YOU as the hero!

ANSWERS

The correct order is: b, d, a, c.

First published in 2011 by
Franklin Watts
338 Euston Road
London
NW1 3BH

Franklin Watts Australia
Level 17/207 Kent Street
Sydney
NSW 2000

A CIP catalogue record for this book is available from the British Library.

ISBN 978 1 4451 0307 5 (hbk)
ISBN 978 1 4451 0315 0 (pbk)

Series Editor: Jackie Hamley
Series Advisor: Catherine Glavina
Series Designer: Peter Scoulding

Printed in China

Franklin Watts is a division of Hachette Children's Books, an Hachette UK company.
www.hachette.co.uk